TOMORROW IS WAITING

written by **Kiley Frank** • illustrated by **Aaron Meshon**

Dial Books for Young Readers

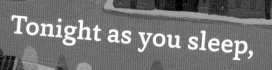

Tonight as you sleep,

a new day stirs.

Each kiss good night

is a wish for tomorrow.

That you'll have wings
enough to fly

as high as   you want.

That you'll explore the world,
only feeling lost in your imagination.

That you'll search with purpose,
laugh with kindness,

act with friendship,

and always know which risks are

worth the courage they take.

As you grow,
I know

there are ancient things
that will speak to you
and whisper wonder
in your ear.

There are first moments
that will dance with you,

and your heart will
unfold and spring.

I know, too,
that there will be injustice
that will challenge you,

and it will surprise you
how brave you can be.

Take time to listen.

Take time to be heard.

Take time to feel small
in the face of something so big.

Tomorrow is waiting to be discovered,

and I wonder what oceans
you will keep in your heart,

what mountains you will stand on,

what shadows you will jump over.

Your world is just beginning

to deepen and grow.

All too soon, you'll need the map
that is written on your heart.

Follow it to unknown places,

and love will meet you there.